The Goblin Princess

Smoky the Dragon Baby

Jenny O'Connor

illustrated by
Kate Willis-Crowley

ff

FABER & FABER

First published in 2016
by Faber & Faber Limited
Bloomsbury House,
74–77 Great Russell Street,
London WC1B 3DA

A CIP record for this book is available from the British Library

Printed in China

978–0571–31658–8

2 4 6 8 10 9 7 5 3 1

MIX
Paper from
responsible sources
FSC® C020056

Items should be returned on or before the last date shown below. Items not already requested by other borrowers may be renewed in person, in writing or by telephone. To renew, please quote the number on the barcode label. To renew online a PIN is required. This can be requested at your local library.
Renew online @ **www.dublincitypubliclibraries.ie**
Fines charged for overdue items will include postage incurred in recovery. Damage to or loss of items will be charged to the borrower.

Leabharlanna Poiblí Chathair Bhaile Átha Cliath
Dublin City Public Libraries

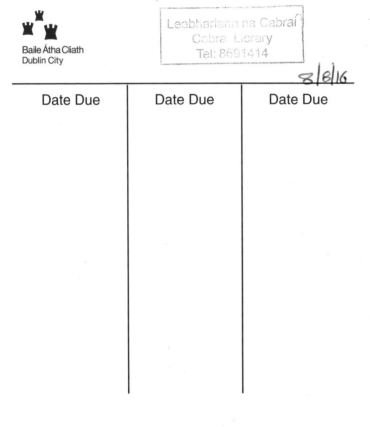

Baile Átha Cliath
Dublin City

8/8/16

Date Due	Date Due	Date Due

For every child who has ever wanted
a pet of their very own.

Chapter 1

The Missing Dragon

In the very top bedroom of the Goblin Castle, Matty, the Goblin Princess, was worried. Posters were spread all around her. Underneath a picture of a large, fat dragon, Matty had written: *Lost! Have you seen this dragon?*

The picture was of Sparks, the adorable but greedy castle dragon, who hadn't been seen since yesterday.

'Sparks has never missed breakfast

2

before. *Someone* must have seen her,' thought Matty, biting her bottom lip. Had the hobgoblins kidnapped her? They had been seen near the castle lately and were known to steal dragons to heat their draughty caves.

'Matty!' screeched the Goblin Queen. Matty's mum came into Matty's bedroom, holding baby Princess Plop. 'Look at the state of this room. It's spotless! It's almost …' she shuddered, '… clean! Untidy it immediately!'

'Plop,' agreed Princess Plop.

'Yes, Mum,' Matty sighed.

Matty knew that she'd let her room get too tidy. She was always getting in trouble for this. Most goblins like their rooms messy, they eat disgusting food and are scared of pretty things like kittens and butterflies. The goblin world is a very upside-down place, and the Goblin Princess never quite felt like she belonged.

'Now, Matty,' said the Queen, 'Mrs Dollop is making some tasty beetle muffins. I'll get her to bring you some up as a special treat.'

'Oh no!' thought Matty. 'I hate beetle muffins more than untidying my room. If only Sparks were here – she'd eat them for me. She loves Mrs Dollop's cooking.'

In the castle kitchen, mice scurried over the kitchen shelves. There were sticky jars of snail slime, dusty packets of spiders' legs, and jars of dead flies, a goblin favourite. Mrs Dollop, the castle cook, was showing Stinkwort, Matty's younger brother, how she made her famous beetle muffins.

'The trick, Stinky, is to add the snail pulp *before* the toadstool flour, then toss in the beetle bits. Delicious!'

Prince
Stinkwort
slyly dipped
a finger
into the
cauldron,
licking his lips.

'Oh, Stinkwort!
If only Matty was a normal goblin like
you and Plop,' fretted the Queen as she
joined them.

'Plop!' agreed Princess Plop.

The Queen sat down and rocked her
baby. 'I'm so worried about Matty.

8

Her room is always tidy and her clothes are spotless. Last week I even caught her combing her hair!'

'It's just an awkward stage. She'll grow out of it, Your Gobness,' comforted Mrs Dollop, as she poured the beetles into her cake mixture. 'Hey, Stinky! Stop eating my beetles!' She swatted away his hand.

Stinkwort picked a flea out his hair, ate that instead, and went back to reading a scary book he had found in the castle library.

'Stinkwort, you shouldn't read

those fairy tales. You'll give yourself
nightmares,' scolded his mother.

Stinkwort giggled. 'Fairies are totally
gross, Mum! With their pretty dresses
and shiny wings. Eurgh!'

'Well, don't you worry your horrible little head about them.' The Queen shuddered. 'Fairies don't really exist. It's just a story to teach youngsters like you to be naughty.'

When Mrs Dollop had taken the cakes out of the oven, she took a little plate of them up to Matty's bedroom. 'Here you are, my little rabbit dropping,' she said. 'I've made you some tasty beetle muffins and a slime shake.'

'Er, thanks, Mrs Dollop,' said Matty.

11

The old cook grinned. 'Oooh, your room looks lovely and messy now. Except, wait a moment …' On Matty's shelf was a neat stack of books.

Mrs Dollop reached up and knocked them to the floor. 'Ah, much better! Now, I'd better get back to the kitchen. I have to make a snail stew for supper.'

Mrs Dollop waddled off, and Matty sighed. 'Oh, Sparks! Where are you? I'd eat all the beetle muffins in Goblin Kingdom if only you were here. I wouldn't even mind my messy room.'

Matty began to nibble a muffin, feeling rather sick as the beetle bits crunched between her teeth.

GRUMPH.

Matty stopped. 'What's that noise?'

GRUMPH.

'There it is again.' Matty put down the muffin.

GRUMPH.

'I think there's something in my wardrobe.' Matty stood up and slowly opened the wardrobe door.

To her astonishment, two eyes peeked out from under her winter

cape. 'Oh, Sparks!' cried Matty. 'I've been so worried, you silly old dragon.'

Sparks lolloped out of the wardrobe and licked Matty's face. 'Hiding!'

'But why, Sparks?' Matty peered into the wardrobe and gasped. There, nestling at the bottom, was a large blue egg. 'So that's what you've been up to, you funny little dragon! You've laid a dragon egg!'

'Pewumf! Egg!' said Sparks proudly.

Matty picked up the egg and stroked it in fascination. 'It's so warm,' she gasped.

At that very moment, the egg moved slightly and then… **CRACK!**

Matty stared as the egg slowly broke open in her hand and a little blue head peeked out. It was a baby dragon!

'Oh, Sparks! Look! You have a beautiful baby! I've always wanted my very own pet dragon.'

'Pewumf?' peeped the baby.

'Sparks, do you think that Dad will let me keep him?' asked Matty. 'Sparks?'

But Sparks was too busy wolfing down the plate of beetle muffins to answer.

Chapter 2

Miss Grimwig

The next morning, Matty brought the baby dragon down to breakfast. 'Look at Sparks's baby! Can I keep him, Dad?' she said, showing off the little dragon to the Goblin King and Queen. The dragon pup peeked shyly out from under Matty's chair at all the noisy

18

goblins eating their breakfast.

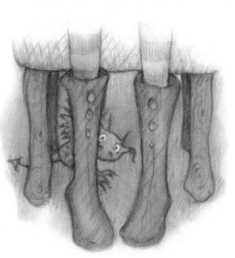

The King looked up from his newspaper and glanced quickly at the dragon. 'Looks much too well behaved to be a pet,' he grunted.

'Oh, not snail porridge again, Mrs Dollop!' complained the Goblin Queen. 'This is the fifth day in a row!'

Mrs Dollop ladled the slimy mixture into their bowls. 'Sorry, Your Gobness.

The toaster's broken again.'

'Plop!' giggled Princess Plop, bashing her spoon in the sticky mixture.

'I *love* snail porridge! It's so slimy!' cried Stinkwort, chucking a spoonful at Matty. She ducked out of the way, but a huge splat of porridge landed on the baby dragon's tiny head.

'Pewumf?' Two little eyes peeked out from the splodge of snail porridge and looked up at Matty.

'Stinkwort! How could you?' Matty lifted the dragon pup up on to her lap

and wiped his face.

'Powwidge,' whimpered the baby dragon.

'Aw, Matty, he's just like you then. Tidy and clean. *Tidy and clean should never be seen,*' chanted her brother. *'Tidy and clean should never be seen!'*

Matty decided to ignore him. 'Dad? *Please* can I keep the baby dragon? I'd *love* a pet of my own.'

The king frowned, put down his newspaper and looked at his daughter. 'You know I'm not keen on the idea of pets, Matty, especially well-behaved

ones. If you want to keep your dragon
pup, he'll have to learn to be messy and disobedient. And you will have to learn how to be an irresponsible pet owner. Every goblin knows that pets should be mucky and wilful.' The king lifted his newspaper. 'Now, as bad luck would have it, here's an article

about a Miss Grimwig, a goblin who can untrain dragons. If you're serious about this, Matty, I'll summon her immediately.'

'Untwain dwagons?' Under the table, the baby dragon pricked up his ears and started to tremble.

The very next day, Miss Grimwig, the dragon untrainer, came marching up the castle path holding a large battered bag. By her side was her huge lolloping dragon called Slobber.

Matty opened the front door.

'H-hello?'

'Ah, hello! You must be Princess Matty,' boomed Miss Grimwig. 'Now, where's that awful, obedient dragon pup I've heard about?'

The poor baby dragon dived headfirst into a plant pot to hide from

the scary woman.
All Miss Grimwig
could see of
her new pupil
was two tiny
quivering legs.
'Ah! Here
he is,' she said,
pulling him
out. Miss Grimwig dangled the baby
dragon upside down up by his feet and
took a good hard look. 'Not promising
material, I must say, but he's just made
his paws muddy in the plant pot, so

that's a good start. Matty, there are three tests to check for naughty dragon potential.

'Test One: Chewing Slippers. Now, young pup, watch Slobber to see how it's done.' Miss Grimwig lifted a pair of slippers out of her large battered bag and threw one to each dragon. In seconds, Slobber had devoured the slipper. **'SLUURRP! BUURRP!'**

'Now, young dragon, you try. Chomp the heel! Chew the sole! Crunch the slipper!'

'Cwunch slipper?' Matty's young

dragon looked shocked at the idea.

'Er, I'm not sure
that chewing
slippers is quite
his thing,' Matty
explained.

'Hmmm,' said Miss Grimwig. 'I
think it's time for Test Two: Ruining
Furniture and General Mayhem.'

She led the two dragons up the tall,
curling staircase to Matty's bedroom.
'Right. Up on the bed with those
horrible paws, you two!'

'Howwible paws!' The little dragon

shook his head and scuttled back
to hide behind Matty's legs.

'This is *RIDICULOUS!*'
bellowed a pink-faced Miss
Grimwig. 'Quickly now! Test
Three is Burning Curtains,
which is Slobber's favourite trick.
Go on, Slobber! Show him how
it's done!'

'Watch this!' growled Slobber,
breathing fire on a curtain. The
fabric caught alight and soon it
was a black mess of ashes.

'Come on, little dragon,' said

Matty, crossing her fingers.

'Slobber's shown you what to do. This is your last chance. *Breathe fire!*' commanded Miss Grimwig.

The little dragon drew in a deep breath, puffed out his tiny pink cheeks and blew. Two small puffs of smoke popped out of his mouth and drifted past Miss Grimwig's long green nose.

'Smoke? *Smoke!* IS THAT ALL YOU CAN DO?!' Miss Grimwig roared at the quivering baby dragon.

She looked so cross that Matty began to giggle.

'This is no
laughing matter,'
said Miss Grimwig as she
packed up her large bag
and stomped down the
long, winding staircase.
'This dragon is a waste
of my valuable time.
I can't do anything with the creature.
You will never be an irresponsible
owner, Princess Matty.'

Slobber took one last withering look

at the baby dragon and followed his mistress down the castle path.

Oh dear. Matty sat on the steps of the castle and cuddled the tiny dragon. 'This is terrible!' she told him. 'When Dad finds out, he'll never let me keep you.'

'Tewwible,' agreed the baby dragon.

Chapter 3

The Royal Family Toaster

Next morning, Matty came down to the kitchen with the little dragon in her arms. 'Hello, Mrs Dollop.'

'A goblin bad morning to you, Matty! The postgoblin has been,' said Mrs Dollop, throwing a handful of letters on to the kitchen table.

'Now, hurry up and eat your breakfast. A little bug has told me that you're going on a picnic today.'

Matty saw to her horror that one of the letters was addressed to the Goblin King and was from the Grimwig Dragon Untraining School.

'Not snail porridge again, I hope, Mrs Dollop!' said the King, coming in and looking suspiciously at the large bubbling cauldron on the cooker.

Mrs Dollop fetched a loaf of bread and started to slice it. 'Well, I'll try the toaster, Your Gobjesty, but I think it's

still broken.'

The King spotted the pile of post on the table. When he opened the letter from Miss Grimwig, his expression grew stern. Next to a picture of the baby dragon was one large word: **FAILED**.

'Oh dear, Matty. In Miss Grimwig's opinion, nothing more can be done with your dragon.

He's too clean, he's too well behaved, and he can't breath fire. He can only make puffs of smoke! I'm afraid he's too good. You won't be able to keep him.'

Matty felt her eyes filling up with tears.

'Ha ha ha! What a rubbish dragon!' scoffed Stinkwort. 'You should call him Smoky!'

Sitting on Matty's lap, the little dragon sucked in his cheeks …

… And blew out a tiny puff of smoke.

'Look at that! Is that the best he can do?' sneered Stinkwort.

'Don't listen to him,' sniffed Matty. 'But Smoky is a good name for you, I have to admit. Can you say my name? My name's Matty.'

'Smatty,' said Smoky, and Matty laughed.

Then the baby dragon drew in a deep breath. His little face grew pink with effort, and suddenly a lick of flame darted across the kitchen table.

'Watch out for the bread!'

cried Mrs Dollop. But it was too late.
The slices were now charred and
blackened.

Matty put her head in her hands.
'Oh, Smoky, you've
ruined breakfast!
I'll never get to
keep you now.'

'Ruined
breakfast?' said
the Goblin Queen.
'What nonsense.
This toast is perfect!
I haven't had toast in ages.'

Mrs Dollop gasped. 'It's true! Each slice has been done to a perfect black crisp. Just the way you like it, Your Gobness.'

The Goblin King was delighted too. 'Well done, Smoky. Fire at the dining table. Very naughty. Good dragon – er, I mean, bad dragon.'

'Bad dwagon! Bad dwagon,' peeped the young dragon proudly.

'C-can I keep Smoky then, Dad?'

asked Matty hopefully.

The King frowned. 'I don't know, Matty.'

'He *does* make good toast,' said the Queen as she chewed.

'Plop,' agreed Princess Plop, munching on a black crust.

'It's true,' said Stinkwort, licking his lips. 'Even if he is a silly baby.'

The Goblin King scratched his chin. 'Well, I'll think about it, Matty.'

'But he can't just be *your* pet, Mats,' laughed Stinkwort, smearing

spider-leg jam on to another piece
of toast. 'Smoky's got a much more
important job – as the Royal Family
Toaster!'

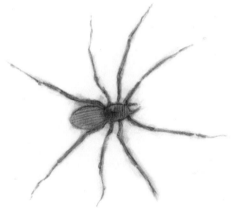

Chapter 4

Dragon Lagoon

Outside it was grey and rainy, the perfect weather for a goblin family picnic at Dragon Lagoon. Mrs Dollop packed the goblins a picnic basket with her frogspawn jelly and special worm pasties, and the family set off for the lagoon.

The goblins found a muddy spot close to the water's edge, and the Goblin Queen unpacked the picnic basket. 'Grub's up!' she cried.

'Plop!' laughed Princess Plop, reaching for a worm that had crawled out from one of Mrs Dollop's pasties.

'Anyone for a jelly?' chortled Stinkwort, throwing a still wiggling frogspawn jelly at his dad.

'That's my boy,' laughed the

King, throwing another back at him.
SPLAT!

Goblins love nothing more than a good food fight, and a really messy one quickly broke out.

'Grub attack!' yelled Stinkwort, throwing a snail pasty at Matty.

'Gwub attack?' whimpered Smoky, hiding behind Matty's legs.

'Don't worry, Smoky. My family are always like this on picnics. We'll go and explore,' Matty said, narrowly dodging a flying pasty. 'Mum, I'm just going to take Smoky for a walk.'

'Well, be back soon,' said the Queen, wiping mud all over Princess Plop's face. 'And remember to be careful! There are hobgoblins about.'

Matty and Smoky set off to explore and soon left the noise of the goblin food fight far behind them. The sun was out, and the lagoon sparkled in the sunlight as the two wandered under the rustling willow trees.

'It's so beautiful, Smoky,' sighed

Matty. There was a splashing sound in
the water, so the two of them wandered
closer. There was something in the
lagoon.

Matty and Smoky knelt down
behind some bushes at the water's edge
and peeked out. There was a family of
wild dragons splashing about in the
water!

'Oh, how sweet,' Matty whispered to
Smoky. 'Young dragon pups, just like
you!'

Smoky wagged his tail happily. 'Dwagons!'

They looked like they were having a lot of fun.

There were some older, larger dragons watching the youngsters from the lagoon's edge and laughing as they splashed and chased each other.

Matty stood up. 'We'd better get back to the picnic. Mum will be wondering where we've got to.'

'Dwagons?' whined Smoky.

'Come on, Smoky,' said Matty. Smoky stared longingly back at

the wild dragons. Then, one of them looked round. 'Rrr-ow?' The dragon smiled at Smoky, and he grinned back at her.

'No. Come on, Smoky,' said Matty, walking quickly away. 'And we had better hurry. I didn't realise how late it was. Look, the sun is going down. I wonder if they have packed up the picnic by now. . . Smoky?' But when Matty turned around, she saw that her little pet dragon wasn't there.

'Smoky?' Matty called. But there was no answer. Just trees rustling.

 50

'Smoky?' Matty called again. 'Are you hiding? I know you're supposed to try and be a bit more naughty, but you can come out now.'

Still there was no answer.

Now Matty was really worried. She tried to retrace her steps back to the lagoon, looking up in the trees and under bushes.

'Smoky! Smoky!' she called, but it was no good.

Smoky didn't
appear. Matty
listened carefully
but she couldn't
hear his little
footsteps or his
dragon pup noises.
'Oh no!' she wailed.
And now the Goblin Princess
suddenly noticed
she was
amongst the
huge trees
of Raven

Wood. Plopping down by a large oak tree to catch her breath, she looked around. 'I've been so busy looking for Smoky that I've taken a wrong turn and now I'm lost.'

BOOM!
BOOOM!
BOOOM!

What was that? Footsteps. Very loud footsteps. And they were coming her way!

Chapter 5

Raven Wood

Matty, terrified, sat very still and listened to the sound of footsteps approaching. Could it be a hobgoblin patrol?

'Hey!' came a tiny voice.

'What was that?'

'Up here.'

Looking up, Matty saw little shimmering glows of light hovering all around her. 'Fairies!' she whispered in amazement. 'So the legend *is* true. They really do exist!'

'You're in danger,' came a tinkly voice. 'We're going to lift you to safety.'

Matty felt herself being lifted upwards by a band of tiny fairies, and soon she was sitting on a tree branch high above the ground.

'Wow!'

'Shhh!' said one of the fairies. 'The hobgoblins are coming.'

Sure enough, a patrol of hobgoblins came marching along the woodland path below.

Matty shuddered. She had never seen a hobgoblin before, but she had heard that they were greasy, grey and wrinkly, and they were famed for their noisy hobnailed boots.

'They're looking for dragons to light fires to heat their caves,' whispered a little fairy who was sitting on Matty's shoulder.

 56

The Goblin Princess looked around in wonder. The tiny fairies fluttered with glittering wings amongst the trees. Their clothes were made of delicate petals and leaves, and they had tiny flowers in their hair.

Now that Matty was safe up on a tree branch, some of the little twinkling fairy lights started to fly away, gradually disappearing into the wood, until only three little sparks remained.

'Have you never seen a fairy before?' said one. 'My name is Fern.'

'We're Tansy and Teasel,' grinned

two cheeky young
twin fairies.

Matty had
always been
taught that fairies
were invisible to
truly naughty goblins,
and if she behaved too much,
she'd be able to see them. But she'd
always thought that was just a story.

'It's true then,' whispered Matty to
the fairies. 'You do exist! And I'm not
like other goblins, or I wouldn't be
able to see you.'

While Matty hid from the hobgoblins in Raven Wood, Smoky was still splashing happily in the lagoon with his new dragon friends.

SPLOSH! The young dragon pups took turns jumping off the waterside rocks. 'Snarf!' This was fun.

'OWW!' One baby dragon pulled Smoky's tail cheekily.

'OOOMPH!' Another dragon jumped on top of him. Smoky dived into the water and swam away from them towards the lagoon's edge.

'Wuff dwagons! Too wuff!' Matty
never pulled his tail or pushed him
over in the water. She was kind and
sweet. Suddenly Smoky longed for his
friend. But where was she?

'Find Smatty!' Smoky climbed out
of the lagoon, sniffed the air and then

the ground. The princess had taken
this path.

The little dragon started following
Matty's scent towards Raven Wood.
'Find Smatty!'

Smoky snuffled and sniffed his way
along the woodland path.

It grew darker and darker as the
trees crowded thickly around him.
The little dragon was now in the
middle of Raven Wood.

It was quiet here. All Smoky could
hear was birdsong and the rustling of
small creatures in the undergrowth.

 63

BOOM!

BOOOM!

BOOOM!

The sudden sound of
hobnailed boots marching
towards him made him stop and
tremble.

'Oh, cwumbs!' he peeped.

High above in the trees, the
fairies were giving Matty a tour
of their world.

'This is where we live,' said
Fern, who seemed to be in
charge. Peeking through a small,
beautifully carved window in
a huge oak tree, Matty could

make out tiny rooms, staircases and tiny wooden furniture.

'Oh, it's beautiful!' she marvelled.

'And that's where we play,' added the twins, Tansy and Teasel.

Looking up into the branches, Matty noticed tiny swings, ropes, little ladders and curved slides.

'Raven Wood is a very magical place,' said Fern proudly.

Teasel and Tansy nodded their heads and grinned shyly up at Matty. They liked the Goblin Princess.

Suddenly they heard shouts on the

woodland path far below them.

'Oh no!' cried Fern.

Looking down, Matty gasped in horror. Two hobgoblins were stomping by on the path below carrying a wooden cage... and in it sat a little dragon, looking miserable and very small.

'Ha ha!' said one hobgoblin. 'This young squirt will be perfect for heating the dungeon kitchens of Hob Mountain.'

'What a find!' chortled the other. 'Nothing like a dragon to cook our

breakfast bacon just how we like it –
flame-grilled and crisp!'

Matty, watching from above, was
appalled. How could those hobgoblins
put her sweet Smoky in that horrible
cage?

'Shhh, we must be quiet.' Fern put her finger to her lips before Matty could cry out.

'Whatever can we do, Fern?' whispered Teasel.

Fern shook her head sadly. 'There's nothing that can be done. What could three fairies and a princess do against two huge hobgoblins?'

'We can't just let them take Smoky,' sobbed Matty. 'I can't bear the thought of him in the dungeon kitchens of Hob Mountain. He's so small and young. He'll hate it.'

'Don't cry, Matty,' comforted Fern. 'We'll think of something.'

The twins, Tansy and Teasel, had been whispering to each other, and suddenly they stepped forward.

'We have a plan,' they declared.

'You two youngsters think you can take on the hobgoblins and rescue Smoky?' scoffed Fern.

 71

'Yes, we can,' said Tansy simply. 'Just watch us.'

Chapter 6

Fairies to the Rescue

Down below, on the forest path, Smoky sat trembling in his little wooden cage. Where were these horrible, loud creatures taking him? 'To Smatty?' he asked the hobgoblins hopefully.

'Not to Smatty, whatever that is,' cackled one hobgoblin.

Matty and Fern watched anxiously from the tree branches. Teasel and Tansy were busy, high up in the oak tree.

'What are you two doing?' called Fern as softly as she could.

'We're collecting acorns,' whispered Tansy.

'You're doing what?' said Fern. 'You think you can save that poor dragon from the hobgoblins with . . . acorns?'

But Teasel and Tansy didn't reply. They had flown down to the lower branches just above the two hobgoblins.

'What are they doing now?' asked Matty, but Fern just shook her head. She didn't know.

Tansy looked up at them and put a finger to her lips. They should all be quiet. Then, she carefully took aim and fired an acorn at one of the hobgoblins.

'OWW!' shouted the hobgoblin, rubbing his head. 'Stop that, Spike! It hurts!'

 75

'I didn't do anything, Trotter,' snapped Spike. Up above, Tansy aimed another acorn at Trotter, while Teasel pelted one at Spike.

'**OWW!** There you go again,' bellowed Trotter.

'**OUCH!** I did not, so don't throw things yourself,' howled Spike.

The hobgoblins dropped the cage

and glared at one another.

Teasel beckoned the other fairies.
'Now's your chance,' she whispered to
Fern.

Fern flew down while the hobgoblins
were busy arguing. Soon, other fairies
flew to join them.

'Look!' gasped Trotter.

Twinkly lights surrounded the cage,
which slowly lifted off the ground.

'A cage just rising up like that for
no reason! I told you these woods were
haunted,' trembled Spike.

The cage hung in the air for a

moment, and then rose up into the oak tree.

'RUN!' The cowardly hobgoblins sprinted off into the trees as fast as their hobnailed boots could carry them.

In his cage, now high above the woodland path, Smoky's eyes widened in delight.

'Smatty?' Was he imagining it? Was that his lovely friend?

'**SMATTY!**' It was!

With trembling hands, Matty released the catch on the wooden cage

and lifted the baby dragon into her arms.

'Oh, Smoky! I didn't think I'd ever see you again!' she cried.

'Hooray!' cheered Tansy and Teasel.

'Well done, you two,' said Fern.

'Thanks. You were both so brave!' said Matty.

'Cwumbs!' Smoky looked around in wonder at the beautiful, tiny fairies.

'You can see them too, Smoky!' cried Matty, astonished.

'Matty,' said Fern, 'you must return to Dragon Lagoon and the picnic. Your parents will be worried.'

'Oh, yes!' Matty gasped. In all the excitement, she'd completely forgotten about the goblin family picnic!

With the sun setting, the fairies
led Matty and the exhausted dragon
through Raven Wood and back along
the path to Dragon Lagoon.

Matty lifted the sleepy dragon
into her arms. 'We're so late, Smoky,'
whispered Matty. 'Dad will be furious.
He'll never let me keep you now.'

'Sowwy, Smatty.'

'I know you are, Smoky. At least
you've been saved from the hobgoblins
and a terrible time in the caves of Hob
Mountain.'

'Goodbye, Matty. Goodbye, Smoky,' chorused the fairies, swooping around them both. 'I'm sure we'll see you again soon.'

'Oh, yes, please!' cried Matty. 'And thank you all for saving my dragon.'

Then, with a shower of sparkles, the fairies flew off into the wood, until all Matty could see were little twinkles in the distance.

The Goblin King and Queen
had already packed up the picnic
things when Matty returned with the
exhausted dragon pup.

'Where have you been, Matty?'

said the Queen
crossly. 'We've
had to pack up
all these things
without you,
and you missed a
wonderful food fight.'

'Sorry, Mum. Smoky ran
off and I got lost looking for him.'

The King chortled and patted
Smoky's sorrowful head. 'Ran off,
did he? There's hope for you yet, you
naughty boy. Miss Grimwig would be
delighted!'

As the family headed for home, the King was thoughtful. At last he spoke. 'Well, I've been thinking, Matty. As Smoky's showing some promise, maybe he *would* be the right kind of naughty pet for you after all.'

Matty looked up with shining eyes. 'D-do you mean I can keep him, Dad?'

'Well, yes,' chuckled the Goblin King. 'I suppose I do!'

That night, Matty went to bed with the sleepy baby dragon snuggled next to her. 'I may not be like all the other

goblins, Smoky,' she whispered, 'but now I'm not alone. I have you as my very own pet dragon, and new amazing fairy friends. We'll have so many exciting adventures together! Sweet dreams, Smoky.'

'Sweet dweams, Smatty!'

COMING SOON...

The Goblin
Princess

at the
GRAND
GOBLIN BALL